the CANMan

Hope lives
—*L.E.W.*

For Roy and Ginny, in appreciation of your hospitality
—*C.O.*

ACKNOWLEDGMENTS

Thanks to the people at Lee & Low Books, who have the talent and heart to match their wonderful vision. It has always been such a pleasure to work with you. —*L.E.W.*

Special thanks to everyone who modeled for the various characters—most especially Jordan Cloutier as Tim, Jason Hommas as Mike, Eleanor Kleiner as Tim's sister, and Charles Sellers as The Can Man. —*C.O.*

Text copyright © 2010 by Laura E. Williams
Illustrations copyright © 2010 by Craig Orback

LEE & LOW BOOKS Inc., 95 Madison Avenue, New York, NY 10016
leeandlow.com
Manufactured in China by Jade Productions
Book design by Kimi Weart
Book production by The Kids at Our House
The text is set in Granjon
The illustrations are rendered in oil on canvas
(hc) 15 14 13 12 11 10 9 8
(pb) 10 9 8 7 6
First Edition

Library of Congress Cataloging-in-Publication Data
Williams, Laura E.
The can man / by Laura E. Williams ; illustrated by Craig Orback. — 1st ed.
p. cm.
Summary: After watching a homeless man collect empty soft drink cans for the redemption money, a young boy decides to collect cans himself to earn money for a skateboard until he has a change of heart.
ISBN 978-1-60060-266-5 (hardcover : alk. paper) ISBN 978-1-62014-577-7 (pbk)
[1. Homeless persons—Fiction. 2. Charity—Fiction. 3. Generosity—Fiction.] I. Orback, Craig, ill. II. Title.
PZ7.W666584Can 2010   [E]—dc22   2009022788

LEE & LOW BOOKS INC.
NEW YORK

the CANMan

by **Laura E. Williams** • illustrated by **Craig Orback**

The homeless man slowly pushed his battered shopping cart down the sidewalk. At the corner trash barrel, he stopped and poked through the garbage with a long stick. He leaned into the barrel and dug out an empty soft drink can, which he dropped into his cart.

As he approached Tim, the man waved. Tim returned the wave with a smile. Almost everyone called the man The Can Man. But not Tim's parents. "We remember when Mr. Peters lived in apartment 3C," Tim's mom told him. "He used to work at the auto body shop before it went out of business, and he couldn't find another job. He's been down on his luck for quite a while now."

"Getting chilly," The Can Man said as he rattled by.

Tim looked at the gray sky. "It sure is," he said. He zipped his jacket up higher and slipped his hands into his pockets.

A few minutes later Mike whizzed up on his skateboard, his cheeks red from the cold. "Want to go skateboarding in the park?" he asked.

Tim shook his head. "Nah. It's no fun always borrowing your board and your brother's old gear."

"Maybe you'll get your own board for your birthday next week."

Tim shrugged. "Dad says we don't have any extra money for toys or sports stuff this year. Too many bills to pay."

"Bummer," Mike said. He kicked away from the steps. "I'll see you later."

Tim watched his friend speed away. Silently, Tim wished for a skateboard for his birthday, even though he knew birthday wishes don't really come true.

ON SALE
STARTING
MONDAY

Tim knew exactly which board he wanted. He had been eyeing it at Overtime Sports for months, and now it was going on sale. But even at the reduced price—and with the money Tim had saved from his allowance—the board was still too expensive.

I need a job, Tim thought glumly, *so I can earn money to buy the skateboard.*

Down the street, The Can Man threw two more cans into his cart. The empties hit the growing pile, clinking like the coins in Tim's little sister's piggy bank. The sound gave Tim an idea.

Early Saturday morning Tim rushed to get dressed. In the kitchen he grabbed a pair of rubber gloves and four big plastic bags from under the sink.

"What are you up to?" his mom asked.

"I have a job to do!" Tim said. Then he added with a grin, "Don't worry. I'll be home in time for lunch."

Outside, the cold air raised goose bumps on Tim's arms. He jumped down the stairs and headed for the first trash barrel on the sidewalk. An empty can lay right on top. After checking several more barrels, Tim had filled half a bag. At five cents a can at the redemption center, he figured he would have enough money for a skateboard in no time.

A few blocks from the park, Tim stopped in to see Jamal at Bunus Bakery.

"Do you have any empty soft drink cans?" Tim asked.

"I usually save them for The Can Man," Jamal said. "He needs them."

"I need them too. I'm going to use the money to buy myself a skateboard for my birthday," Tim told Jamal. "I'll even work to earn the cans."

"Well . . ." Jamal hesitated for a few moments. "Maybe this one time. I do have some crates you can carry to the back room."

"It's a deal!" Tim replied.

After he had moved the crates and collected the cans as payment, Tim ran down the street, stopping at every trash barrel, store, and restaurant. By noon he had two full bags of cans. He clattered them up the stairs of his building and plopped down on the top step.

Collecting cans was harder than Tim thought it would be. His gloves were sticky, and his clothes smelled like the root beer he'd spilled on himself. But the thought of a brand-new skateboard made him smile. Very soon he'd have one of his own. No more borrowing Mike's board.

"What do you have there?" Tim's mom asked when he dragged the bags into the kitchen.

"They're full of cans for recycling. I'm earning money for a skateboard."

"Doesn't Mr. Peters usually collect the cans around here?" his mom asked.

Tim nodded uneasily. "Yeah. But I'm only going to take them until my birthday."

"Well, you can't keep them in here," his mom said. "Take them to the basement, and then wash up for lunch."

Tim knew it was no use arguing, so he bumped the bags downstairs to the basement. They crackled and clanked with every step.

Sunday after church, Tim hurried from one stinky trash barrel to the next, collecting empty cans. For the rest of the week, he had to wait until after school. Tim knew The Can Man always took the same route, so he started in the opposite direction. That way he got to some of the trash barrels before The Can Man did.

On Saturday Tim awoke to icy drizzle squiggling down his window. With a groan, he dragged himself out of his warm bed and into the kitchen.

Tim's dad patted him on the shoulder. "Sorry, Tim," he said. "It looks like you'll have to stay indoors today."

"But this is my last chance to collect cans," Tim protested. "I can't let a little rain stop me."

His dad looked out the window. "Okay, but don't stay outside too long."

On the sidewalk, Tim poked through a few trash barrels. The rain made the garbage smell even worse than usual, and there wasn't a single can to be found.

Keeping his face down to shield it from the cold rain, Tim ran toward the next trash barrel.

Thwump!

Tim jerked up his head. "Oh, sorry!" he exclaimed.

"You okay, kid?" The Can Man asked.

"Yeah. Sure." Tim looked into the cart. All he saw was an old bucket of paint and a few empty soft drink cans. The rain pinged on them hollowly.

"Haven't found many cans lately," The Can Man said, poking his stick into the trash barrel. "How are you doing? I've seen you out collecting."

"I have seven bags full of them at home."

"Seven?" The Can Man said, his eyes wide.

"My birthday is tomorrow," Tim explained. "I'm going to use the money to buy a skateboard. What are you collecting for?"

The Can Man shrugged. "Wouldn't mind a new coat before the snow starts flying."

Tim swallowed. "Oh."

"Well, kid, see you around." The Can Man pushed his cart down the sidewalk, his ripped jacket flapping open with every step.

When the rain stopped, Tim called Mike. Then Tim dragged his bags of cans from the basement to the front of his building. He sat on the steps to wait.

Mike rolled up on his skateboard. "Looks like you'll have enough for a board once you turn in these cans," he said.

Tim nodded. "I guess so."

The boys looked up as the clatter of The Can Man's cart came toward them. The Can Man stopped at the bottom of the stairs. "You need help with your bags?"

"Okay," Tim said.

They loaded the bags into the cart, and The Can Man pushed it while Tim and Mike kept the pile from toppling over.

At the redemption center, it took a long time for Tim and Mike to push all the cans into the machine. Tim collected his coins in a paper bag he had brought along.

By the time the boys were done depositing the cans, The Can Man had left. Tim looked outside. Small flakes of snow were sprinkling down from the sky, lightly dusting the parking lot. He shook the bag that held his money. The coins rattled like a cart full of empty cans.

Suddenly Tim headed outside.

"Hey, where are you going?" Mike called after him.

Tim ran and caught up with The Can Man. Holding out the bag of coins, Tim said breathlessly, "This money is for you."

The Can Man stared in surprise. "But you earned it. You worked hard for your money."

"It's okay," Tim said. "I want you to have it."

The Can Man blinked a few times as though snowflakes had blown into his eyes. "Thanks, kid. What's your name anyway?"

"Tim," Tim said.

"Thanks, Tim. My name's Joe Peters," The Can Man said, smiling.

"I know," Tim said. "My mom and dad remember you from when you lived in our building."

The Can Man's smile faded. "That was a long time ago." He sighed. Then he shook the bag of coins. "Thanks again."

"You're welcome," Tim said.

When he got home, Tim plunked down on the front steps of his building. So he wouldn't get a skateboard for his birthday, but somehow it didn't matter that much anymore.

The next day, wearing new birthday jeans, Tim wandered outside to wait for Mike. On the top step, Tim's foot bumped into a large plastic bag. It was tied closed with a long string attached to an empty root beer can. Tim lightly kicked the bag. Something was in it. He untied the string and peeked inside.

"A skateboard!" he gasped.

Tim slowly ran his hands over the painted wood and spun the wheels. The skateboard wasn't new, but it was fixed up with a fresh coat of paint and oiled wheels. It even had his name painted neatly across the bottom.

Just then Tim heard the rattle of The Can Man's cart. As he approached, The Can Man looked up and waved.

"Happy Birthday, Tim," he called.

Grinning, Tim waved back with his new skateboard. "Thanks, Mr. Peters. Thanks a lot!"